Darling,
LET'S GO & BRING OUR
CHILDREN HOME!

OLUFUNKE OVIAWE

"DARLING, LET'S GO & BRING OUR CHILDREN HOME!"

ISBN: 978-1-9196195-0-7 Paperback

Published by LEXOID Publishing
London. United Kingdom

For information:
olufunkeoviawe@yahoo.co.uk,
olufunkeoviawe@gmail.com

Printed in the United Kingdom

Unless otherwise stated, all scriptures are taken from the New King James Version of the Holy Bible.

DEDICATION

It is with great pleasure that I dedicate
this book to my loving husband,
Pastor Alex Oviawe, and my four precious children.
You all mean the world to me.

TABLE OF CONTENTS

ACKNOWLEDGMENTS

A deep gratitude to the Almighty God, the giver of life, and every good thing. To Him alone be all the glory, and adoration.

In loving memory of the two most beautiful women in my life; My mom, Mrs Rhoda Oladunni Dare, and my sister, Mrs Olanike Opawoye, I miss you both so much, but I imagine you smiling and nodding your heads saying well done, girl!

Special thanks to my uncle, and big brother, who has always looked after me, Mr Ayodele Thomas, and my elder brother, Mr Dele Dare.

Special thanks to my sister, and friend, Pastor (Mrs) Funmi Kola-Okeowo, I thank God for your life. Thank you for your enthusiasm, time, support, and belief in the story. I sincerely appreciate your contributions in making the book a reality.

Personal thanks to Pastor & Pastor (Mrs) Odedoyin, Mr. Evans Amoah-Nyamekye, Mr. H.S Kang, Folashade Adeosun, Mrs Efua Ampofo, Pastor Tayo Oladeru, Mrs Bunmi Adebayo-Tandoh, Mrs Rachel Ogiesewu, Mr & Mrs Oyekanmi, Mrs Mabel Fadoju and Mrs Stella Dare for your prayers, support and friendship.

My heartfelt gratitude to every member of RCCG Joint Heirs Connections, and More Than Conquerors Praying forum, for your continuous prayers, and support.

A big thank you to all my siblings.

As always, thanks, and much love to my husband, Alex Oviawe, who does so much for me, and our wonderful children. I love you all.

CHAPTER ONE

Darling, Let's go, and bring our children home! Fred's voice boomed from downstairs. "Don't mind those people, they don't know what they are doing." Said Tola's husband, Fred. Tola walked slowly down the stairs, and as soon as she reached the bottom of the stairs, Fred held out his hand to her, and pulled her into a tight embrace. "You okay?" Fred asked, as he led his wife outside to where he parked his car. Tola nodded her head, and leaned into his chest.

They then drove to the Social Services office, hoping to bring their children back home with them. On their way in the car, while Fred was driving, he tried to reassure his wife in his usual optimistic way, that everything was going to be okay. Tola thereafter felt a glimpse of hope after many hours of crying, and uncertainty. The Social Services' office is located within the Local Authority of London borough of Harlem. It was about a twenty minutes' drive from the family house, but the whole journey seemed like eternity.

Harlem borough is characterised by diverse cultures, and different ethnic groups. These groups range from Pakistani, White British, Black African, Indian, and Other Whites. Houses are relatively cheaper to rent there compared to other boroughs in the city of London. Fred and his family came to live in the borough in March 2007, thereby making them live in Harlem for a total of four years. In Fact, that is the only borough that they have ever resided since migrating to the United Kingdom from Nigeria. Harlem is centrally located as other parts of London can be easily accessed from there, especially if one decides to travel for job opportunities, and employment.

By the time they reached the social Services' office, it was already nearing the closing time, and most of the staff had closed for the day. Nevertheless, both Fred and Tola were directed by the receptionist to the Manager's office, who introduced herself as Mrs Bains, she was of Asian descent.

"Hello Mr and Mrs Thomas, how are you holding up?" "We are good, thank you", replied Fred while Tola nodded her head, and whispered, "thank you" quietly.

"I'm sorry we are meeting under such a challenging circumstance. A referral was made from your children's school (Broadyard Primary School) this afternoon, for the Local Authority to accommodate your children." Mrs Bains further stressed that she did not know the full story of what transpired in the children's school, but said the Local Authority had contacted a foster carer to put children up for the night. However, she advised Tola and Fred to call and speak to friends and family, who could accommodate their children in the foreseeable future while the Local Authority will be conducting their investigations. The Thomas' family's parental responsibility had been inadvertently withdrawn from them, and both Fred, and Tola went back home, heartbroken, and confused.

They could not believe what had just happened. Hence, this began a conundrum with the Social Services, and the Police, which will last for over a year.

Everything that happened was already determined long ago, and we all know that you cannot argue with someone who is stronger than you. **Ecclesiastes 6:10 (Good News Translation)**

Earlier that same day on the 20th of October 2011, the Thomas' family woke up that particular day, and had their family morning devotion as usual, by singing worship songs, praying, and reading the Bible.

Thereafter, they laid hands on their children, and pronounced blessings upon them. Fred then left for his office; he always leaves early to avoid the traffic. Tola bathed the children, and got them ready for school. Afterwards, she took them to school.

Tola always walks with her four boys (Jameson, nine years old; Jadon, seven; Joshua, four; and fifteen-months old Justin, strapped in his stroller) alongside a neighbour's son, Derrick, to school every day. Tola became acquainted with Derrick's mum, Yvonne Mensah through her son, Jadon. Jadon and Derrick were in the same class. Tola became friends with Yvonne, when their children (Jadon and Derrick) were in year one, and became closer when Yvonne and her husband Mr Mensah and family moved to the street where the Thomas' family were living.

The Mensah family was originally from Ghana. They were indeed a very nice, and quiet couple. Yvonne sometimes baked cakes for the Thomas' family, and both families enjoyed sharing food recipes. When Yvonne gave birth to her second child, Blessing, and Tola had her youngest son Justin, both of them made an arrangement for Tola to take the children to the school in the morning, while Yvonne picked them from the school in the afternoon.

Later that afternoon, Yvonne suddenly rushed to Tola's house to inform her that when she attempted to pick up Tola's children from their various classes, she was directed by one of the teachers to go and see the Headteacher. Wondering what was wrong; she made her way to the school reception, and asked for the Headteacher, Mr Alexandra. The Headteacher later informed her that it was a confidential matter which could not be discussed with her.

While Yvonne was still narrating her experience, the phone buzzed, and when Tola glanced at the screen, she realised it was from her children's school and she answered. "Hello", Tola got a response, "This is Broadyard School, can I speak to Mrs Thomas?"

"Speaking," she replied.
"Can you please come to the school office immediately?"
"I will be there soon"

Tola quickly roused her youngest son Justin, from his afternoon nap, and Yvonne volunteered to drive them to the school so that it would be faster. The pair were both perplexed, and curious as to what could be the problem.

As soon as Yvonne found a parking space, Tola stormed out of the car, and ran to the office. Unfortunately, she was not allowed to see her children; rather, she was informed by the Headteacher, Mr Alexander that the Social Services from the local Children's Services had taken them away because the children made an allegation of maltreatment against her husband, and herself (the children's parents). She was also told that the Police had been called, and that they would like to speak with her.

Two Police officers then approached her, and asked, "Where is the youngest child? We have been reliably informed that there is another child who was not in school with his siblings."

"He is with my friend in the car outside the school premises," Tola replied. The two police officers then followed Tola to the car and informed her that they would be taking Justin away too, because he was no longer safe with her. By this time Tola had started crying, and her little boy was also crying. Justin was not used to people carrying him apart from his family members, so he was really howling when the Police woman took him from his mother. Tola tried to plead with the Police officer, to allow her to follow them to the place where they were taking him, knowing fully well that once he is reunited with his siblings, he would calm down, but she refused blatantly.

One of the Police Officers said "it's better for him to scream, and cry now than to be abused, I understand that you people mistreat your children in the country where you came from." They said they were going to take him to where his siblings were, and drove him away in the Police car. It was heart-breaking, Tola does not think she could ever get over the experience of a Police officer taking Justin away from her, it will always remain with her as long as she lives. She even had to ask the Police Officer if she had any child of her own, because she handled the whole situation without human feelings, she did not show any empathy despite the age of the child involved.

Yvonne tried her best to console Tola, and then drove her to the house without her children. On reaching the house, she encouraged Tola to take things easy, and left her to have some time to herself alone. Tola paced the living room alone. As expected, she was very tired emotionally, and confused, she decided to call her husband, Fred, who was still at work. When he answered his phone, he told her that the school had already called him, and that he was on his way home. Subsequently, Tola brought out a piece of paper and wrote down the promises of God about children that she knew off hand, whilst she waited for her husband's arrival.

All your children shall be taught by the LORD, And great shall be the peace of your children. **Isaiah 54:13**

CHAPTER TWO

F red told some of his colleagues at work about what had just happened, and one of them said "it's a rampant event now, especially among the African community in London." He also spoke with the school to convince them, saying: "there must be a misunderstanding somewhere." He was so sure that it was going to be a walk in the park, and the crisis would blow over soon. Consequently, he was so confident that they were going to get their children back as soon as they went to the social services office.

As the future is beyond our knowledge and control, it is wise to make the best of the present. Known to God from eternity are all His works. **Acts 15:18**

The following day, Fred and Tola were both distraught because they wouldn't allow them to see their children. Nobody told them anything apart from the fact that an allegation had been made against them by their children. Nothing was further explained aside from the fact that the children had been placed with a foster family who will be looking after them henceforth. They were in a state of utter stupefaction, they didn't really understand what was happening to them. It was hard, and hurtful indeed!

All kinds of thoughts, and ideas were passing through the minds of Fred and Tola, but none could be carried out by them. Their children were now under an authority beyond them. Eventually, they came up with something as a possible ease of tension; Fred and Tola regularly drove round the school in the morning hoping to catch a glimpse of the children at the entrance of the school, unfortunately, they never saw them. They often went back in the afternoon during the school closing hour, and waited in their car by the school gate, but the wait was extremely long, and frustrating because they went back home terribly disappointed daily. Suddenly, on one fateful afternoon, they saw an elderly Caucasian woman (probably in her late 70s, they never really got around to find out), staggered down the road, flanked on both her right and left side by Joshua and Jadon respectively, while Jameson was on the left side of Jadon.

They saw the backs of their children while being escorted by this elderly woman (who they later got to know as Penny) to board a waiting vehicle. Straight away, they felt relieved a little bit that the children were okay, although they didn't see Justin. Apparently, he was with the foster carer, who would later be known as Aunt Bridget. Penny was the one who usually accompanied the children to and from school from the foster carer's home. They had a consistent cab driver that does the school run i.e., both pick up and drop off. Tola and Fred went to the school the following day to further have a peep at their children. They felt angry, overwhelmed and worried for their children's safety and wellbeing as the children were never separated from them before. They have always been a closely knit family whereby they went everywhere with their children.

This was a very little solution to their big problem, but it wasn't going to last as expected. By the fourth day, one of the teachers who knew Tola very well reported to the Social Services that they could see the parents hanging around the school premises. Consequently, the Social Services warned Tola and Fred to desist from going to the school area. They just wanted to make sure that their children were doing okay, and sadly, they were deprived again. Would they have kidnapped their own children? Definitely not, but they ended up stopping them from moving close to the school gate. Fred and Tola still didn't understand why the school, and the Social Services were making a mountain out of a molehill!

In the multitude of my anxieties within me, Your comforts delight my soul. **Psalm 94:19**

In retrospect, if anyone had told Tola that she would give birth to four children in her life, she would have found it difficult to believe. Although she had always loved a big family, because she came from one, she was thinking in the line of two children, or at most, three. However, Fred told her that he wanted four children when they were still courting, and she remembered asking him, what would happen if she could not give birth? He simply reassured her saying, "don't you worry, you will surely give birth." And to the glory of God, Tola got pregnant the same month the couple got married. One after the other the children kept coming. Fred and Tola knew, and appreciated that they are gifts from God. They are heritage from the Lord who should be held in sacred trust.

Tola and Fred met for the first time at work. Immediately after Tola's one-year mandatory service to her country, Nigeria (i.e., National Youth Service Corps), she got a job at a bank, known as Tropical Chartered Bank, it was one of the four leading banks in Nigeria at the time. During this period, Tola was in a relationship with another guy, who she was not really keen about. However, because most of her friends were either married, dating, or in a courtship, she decided to get on with the relationship but she did not consider it a serious one.

When Tola set eyes on Fred for the first time, she'd felt attracted to him, and thought in her heart, "he's probably married, all the handsome men in Lagos were either married, or engaged." Tola had always been romantic at heart, and she saw in Fred all the qualities she desires in a man; a kind and handsome man with a broad shoulder where she could always lay her head upon. She then fell in love. Loving Fred was effortless, he was easy going. Fred was a born-again Christian like her, he dressed well, and was single. What's not to like? Fred was one of the managers at the office, but not her direct boss. The relationship developed very quickly as they saw each other every day at work, and spent time together.

During lunch times, he would take her out for meals, and they also spent time together after work; attending church services on Sundays, going to the beach and cinema etc. Fred had just come out of a long-term relationship, which did not work for him. He was the one that ended his prior relationship, and for that reason, he did not want to waste time, or delay, so he proposed quickly, and Tola accepted with some reservations because Fred was not of the same cultural, and ethnic background like herself: his family was from Benin city and they speak Edo language whilst Tola came from the Yoruba ethnic group with Yoruba being her native language. Fred however speaks both languages. Tola's family initially raised some concerns with regard to the cultural differences amongst both families; they were, however, pleased that Fred was a

Christian, and from a Christian family. Furthermore, they recognised how much in love the couple was.

Tola Thomas was born as Tola Olushola on 28th July 1974 to her parents Olubunmi Olushola born on 15th march 1937 and father Chief Akinwumi Olushola born on 25th of May 1929. Tola was born in Ibadan, Nigeria, at Harmony Hospital, a medical facility jointly owned by her parents. Her father diversified into other areas of businesses like Real estates, and Car Dealership, while her mother worked as both Matron and Midwife at Harmony Hospital. Tola was the fifth child of a sibling group of six (Three boys and three girls in that order). She had a wonderful relationship with both of her parents and siblings, she was living with one of her senior brothers as at the time she met Fred in Lagos. Both parents were very affectionate, hardworking, generous, and God-fearing.

They worked hard to provide for their family, and ensured that all their children were graduates. At a point in time, Tola's father became the president of the rotary club, and he was able to travel with her mum extensively around Nigeria and also to the United Kingdom, and Canada. On their return back home, they always bought gifts for their children.

Fred was born as Fred Thomas on the 23rd October 1968 in Lagos, Nigeria. His mother was Esther Thomas who passed away in 2003 at the age of 72 years, and his father was Francis Thomas who passed away in

1985 at the age of 70 years. Fred was the third child of a sibling group of four brothers. Fred's father worked as an insurance broker before his demise while his mother had a shop that dealt in children's clothing, and toys. Fred's parents were average income earners, but they were comfortable, and able to meet their financial obligations without any major difficulty.

He was also raised with the fear of God by a closely knit family, who loved their children very much. Fred was close to both his parents, and siblings. His parents cherished, and valued educational opportunities for all their children, and they made sure Fred and his siblings received the best education which they could afford. Fred and Tola were the second to the last born of their parents, each of them has a younger brother and sister respectively that looks up to them, and they in return look out for them by giving them gifts. They also provided counselling for them during their relationship period and career.

When Tola announced to her family that they wished to get married after five months of courtship, her family's initial view was that their courtship was too short, and that they did not know each other well enough.

However, Tola was able to convince them otherwise by explaining that they had spent considerable amounts of time together and knew each other exceptionally well. They got married in November 2001 on a bright sunny morning at St Joseph Anglican Church Ibadan, followed by a reception, and all-night party afterwards. The white wedding was preceded by a traditional engagement ceremony, which was a well-attended grand affair that was graced by family and friends followed by thanksgiving at the Apostolic Church in Lagos.

I am my beloved's, and his desire is toward me.
Songs of Solomon 7:10

CHAPTER THREE

Tola cherished her relationship, and marriage immensely. She considered herself blessed, and fortunate to be married to a God-fearing man, who was gentle in every way. Actually, according to Tola, "there is nothing he cannot do for me, and the children. He loves me and his children with a passion." Tola considers Fred to be a friend, and a confidant, and Fred saw her too in the same light.

Fred sees his relationship with his wife, Tola as the only significant relationship he has ever had. All his other relationships, prior to meeting Tola, paled into insignificance. He met Tola when they were both working at the Tropical Chartered Bank head office Apapa, Lagos. Initially he considered her as a fellow co-worker, however, friendship subsequently developed, and from there, their relationship started. Fred saw so many qualities he cherished in a wife in Tola: Tola was

God-fearing, kind hearted and beautiful with a good sense of humour. As a result, Fred fell in love with her very quickly. He remembered teasing her that he was more in love with her than she was with him. During this period, Tola found it difficult to properly pronounce his surname but he kept badgering her that; "You will bear that name when we eventually get married". Fred found something he had never found with anyone else, and they enjoyed each other's company. He loved her passionately, and always desired her to be in his presence.

He also considered their wedding to be a very great and fun day. Fred classified his relationship, and marriage as being exemplary. The marriage was based upon Godly principles of love, affection, and unity. Fred viewed himself, and Tola as being role models for families, and couples. Although He is not perfect; he always hates confrontation while Tola likes to talk things through, but over the years they have learnt to put the interest of each other first. However, there is always room for improvement, and development in any relationship.

The fear of God in the life of a potential spouse is very important when considering a marriage partner. The job title of a partner should not be the only attraction in a relationship as it may not be sustainable because that partner can lose his job. Beauty is a seasonal friend; it always walks away from one eventually. However, a partner that fears the Lord will act in line with God's principles.

Most men will proclaim each his own goodness, But who can find a faithful man? **Proverbs 20:6**

Even though Fred and Tola had a hectic work life at the bank after their wedding, and it continued even after they began to have children, they prioritized the wellbeing of their children by putting their interest at the forefront. They had a house help at home who helped to look after the children. Both the paternal, and maternal mothers came to visit regularly in order to spend time with them, and assist the house help to look after the children when the couple were at work. After a while, the paternal grandmother moved in to live with them until she died.

At weekends, the couple devoted their time, and resources to the joy and happiness of their children: they took them to church; they went shopping; they went out for meals and during holidays they took them to places of interest where they could have fun and also learn the history of Nigeria. They travelled on vacation to the Obudu Mountain Resort in Cross River State, The Royal Palace of Oba of Benin in Edo State, Coconut Beach in Badagry, Lagos State to mention a few. It is indeed a fact that Fred enjoys travelling, and exploring. Pictures were often taken to cherish, and preserve all these wonderful memories with the children.

Jameson was the first child among the four boys of the family. He is a reserved, and quiet boy. He likes to keep to himself, he is easy-going, obedient, very intelligent, and likes to read a lot. Jameson was always protective of his siblings; he enjoys being a big brother, and helps to look after his siblings. He can't stand his siblings being upset.

Tola gave birth to Jameson in Lagos, Nigeria. She didn't even know she was pregnant, having just started her banking career as a cashier at the Tropical Chartered Bank in Lagos; she kept on vomiting all over the place, it was one of the auditors at the bank that told her she was probably pregnant. She could not hold any food down; she would vomit at the cafeteria in front of staff, vomit at the counter in front of customers. Her experience was not just morning sickness, she was vomiting all the time i.e., morning, afternoon, evening, and it was usually accompanied with serious body weakness. Fred took proper care of her during this challenging period. He would hold her, pet her and speak gently to her. He would also be the one to cook and clean the whole house. Tola's best friend, Ranti, who lived on the same estate with her would bring food, but unfortunately, she could not hold any food down.

Tola and Ranti attended the same boarding secondary school, and also attended the same University. Ranti got married while they were still at the University, and lived with her husband and three children on the same estate as Tola. When it seemed as if the vomiting was not abating, Tola decided to take some time off work.

Many of her friends and family members even advised her against taking time off because she had just started her banking career then, but she had already fallen in love with the little baby growing inside her. She cared more about the little life developing inside her than her lucrative job. God granted her favour, with the help of a loving uncle at the executive level of the bank, she was given some time off work without pay until she gave birth.

Jameson's birthing process was very easy to the glory of God. It was as described in the Bible; giving birth like the Hebrew women. It was the Lord's doing, and was marvellous in their eyes. Tola's mom had come over from Ibadan to stay with her in Lagos. She, being a midwife, examined her first before driving her to the hospital. Tola could recollect the first few days after giving birth to her son. Whenever her son cried, it would be as if her heart was breaking in pieces. She would experience this strange sensation all over her body. There was even a particular day she started crying and shouting, thinking something negative had happened to Jameson. Although Tola's mum; being a nurse, later educated her properly that she might have suffered from postnatal depression. However, she didn't know at the time; rather, she just wanted to protect and take care of her son.

Jadon was the second beautiful son of the family. He was an extrovert by nature. He was quite outspoken, comical, full of life and never afraid to express himself.

He could indeed be described as a people-person, very lively, and everyone loved him immensely. He was also very intelligent, and usually asked a lot of questions, and was inquisitive. He was a very nice, and selfless person, always willing to share, and very thoughtful. He looked up to Jameson and if he likes a person, he will always want to do things to please that person. He was born in Lagos, Nigeria as well. His pregnancy was not as difficult as Jameson's. Tola worked throughout his pregnancy period, however, the birthing process was really painful because of inducement.

Happy is the man who has his quiver full of them; They shall not be ashamed, But shall speak with their enemies in the gate. **Psalm 127:5**

CHAPTER FOUR

A few days after the children were taken into care, the Local Authority called Tola, and informed her that they were willing to release the children back to her custody, having interviewed the children by themselves and they did not say anything incriminating against her. However, the police had instructed them not to carry out their intentions of releasing the children. Consequently, the waiting continued. After a couple of weeks, Tola received an impromptu visit from the Police, and they began to search the entire family house looking for weapons of cruelty (as she will later discover) but they did not find anything that remotely resembled what they were looking for. She was then scheduled to attend an interview with the Police.

On the appointed date, Tola travelled to the Police station with her husband, and an associate, called

Susan. Susan didn't just reside in the same geographical area with the couple, but she attended the same church fellowship with them. She went along to offer her moral support. They arrived at the venue earlier than the set time. They therefore decided to hang around the Police station. While they waited, Susan told them different stories of people whose children had been taken into the care system. She said "Brother Fred and sister Tola, do you know that if you decide to have another child now, social services will still take the child from you, as you will be deemed as unfit parents." Tola did not say anything, but her mind kept drifting to what the Police could possibly be interviewing her about.

Eventually, fifteen minutes afterwards, she was seated in an interview room, where a police officer introduced herself as officer Gabriella, while another officer stood by.

"Do you need a lawyer?" asked the officer.

"No, I'm good at answering questions by myself."

Although the whole incident was still new to Tola, notwithstanding, she was so sure that she had done nothing wrong. She has always been a truthful person to the point of being naive at times. The truth can sometimes be very expensive to the extent that it can cost you people, and things you never imagined in your life. So, she told the Police officers that she was good to answer their questions without the presence of a lawyer. They then proceeded to ask various questions ranging from how she disciplines her children to what the word 'beat' really connotes, and about corporal punishment. She was allowed to leave thereafter.

That was when it first dawned on Tola the kind of dilemma she was battling with. Prior to this moment, nobody had bothered to explain anything whatsoever to her. Life altering moments don't usually announce themselves, they just happen suddenly. What she never planned for, or envisaged began to unfold and the whole matter started to spiral out of her control. As a result, she became incapable of controlling all the activities that were happening around her as things began to crop up one after the other, and one humiliating experience after another.

The following week, Fred received a call from DC Police officer, Gabriella, requesting him to come over to the police station for an interview concerning some allegations made against him. Fred therefore reported at the Police station, and waited for about an hour before DC Gabriella arrived in the company of another Police officer. Contrary to what he was told on the phone (i.e., to come for an interview at the police station) and to his uttermost surprise, he was immediately arrested and detained in custody. Thus, it seemed as if he was deceived into coming to the Police station because the officers treated him in a way and manner which gave an impression as if he was not the one who voluntarily came to the station by himself, but was coerced to the station.

Shortly after that, he was led to the prison cell without any explanation while the two police officers went to the family house for a house search without his knowledge. He was left in the prison cell like a common criminal for over three hours without any explanation or a legal representative, probably to intimidate him. When eventually the two Police officers returned from his house, he was brought out of the prison cell, and introduced to a rather strange solicitor who told him that he will represent him during his interview proceedings.

During the interview session with the police officers, some racist and stigmatised comments were made towards Fred by DC Gabriella whereby she said "I am aware that it is part of your culture in Nigeria to be cruel to your children by beating them with objects." Fred immediately replied to her wrong generalisation by educating her that Nigeria is a country with multi-faceted culture, and she should specify which of the cultures she was referring to. Moreover, no Nigeria culture encourages or supports child cruelty. It was obvious that this attitude of DC Gabriella was not only racist, but indeed prejudicial, and judgemental. Consequently, her motives, and actions were subject to questioning, especially with regards to her ability to carry out her investigation with fairness and objectivity. Moreover, contrary to the Police officer's unfounded assertion, Nigerian parents derive real joy in taking proper care of their children. They see children as their joy, and pride. Actually, Fred could recall when Tola gave birth to their children, it was indeed a time of extreme satisfaction, and self-fulfilment.

That was why when the opportunity to travel out of the country arose, they felt it would give their children the best possible privileges life could offer them. Fred first heard about the Highly Skilled Migrant Programme (HSMP) from one of his neighbours, Mr Omotosho while they were chatting during one of the Environmental Sanitation exercises in their local community. Environmental Sanitation is a monthly exercise that is carried out in Nigeria, whereby people basically clean their environment. This exercise usually brings about an avenue for men to chat with one another while they sip orange juice. More so, no movement was permitted in the entire State until after ten o'clock in the morning.

After the exercise, Fred decided to do more research about the HSMP. Having travelled to the UK on holidays before, he felt the UK is a place he could live with his family. Hence, he decided to apply for the HSMP with his wife, and two children (dependents). Fortunately, within a period of three months, he got a favourable response, and was granted a settlement visa.

The Highly Skilled Migrant Visa was as at then, the easiest way to obtain British citizenship in the United Kingdom. The recipient (with his or her family) comes in with a one-year visa, then renew it for another three years, after which he or she will be given 'an indefinite leave to remain', which enables him/her to claim all the privileges that a British citizen is entitled to such as housing benefits, child benefits etc and lastly, the recipient is then permitted to apply for British citizenship within the first year of receiving 'indefinite leave to remain' or thereafter as he/she so desires.

Initially, Fred thought he would go to the UK first, and then come back for the family. However, Tola had become pregnant again, and he decided not to leave her behind. Therefore, Tola and Fred resigned from their lucrative and well-paid jobs. They also left friends and family (they moved away from the known and ventured out to the unknown). By doing so, they ventured into a different culture with the hope that their children's future would be better for it.

Tola was four months pregnant with their third child, when they left the shore of Nigeria to the UK. On their arrival, they stayed with one of Tola's brothers who had been living in the UK for several years with his wife Linda and four children. They welcomed them warmly. Tola's brother, Tunji had been living in Bronx, a northern part of London for over fifteen years. However, Fred preferred the eastern part of London. Consequently, after staying with his in-law for a week, he got his family a rented accommodation in the eastern part of London. Settling into the UK to the standard envisaged took a while because the first four years of their settlement visa had no recourse to public funds, and Fred could not get a job immediately. He was always turned down for his lack of UK working experience, but eventually he was able to register with a recruitment agency which provided him with temporary jobs. The situation was compounded because Tola was pregnant with Joshua, and could not work. However, Tola and Fred did their best to provide for their children within their limited financial resources. At one point, they even had to liquidate some of their investments back home in Nigeria and transferred the money to the UK in order to ease the financial pressure they were then experiencing.

Joshua's birth came with some complications, the umbilical cord was wrapped around his neck three times and he was getting weak. But God intervened at the right time, and Tola still went ahead to have a normal delivery. For the first time Tola was all alone without her mum in the labour ward. Fred had to take Jameson and Jadon to his in-laws to be looked after so that he could go to work since he could not afford to take time off.

Joshua is the third beautiful son of the family. He was a boisterous little boy who could be perceived by others as negative. Due to the fact that he was big for his age, people have high expectations of him. He was full of energy, and loved to play a lot. He also usually takes pleasure in dancing, and exerting his energy. However, on a down side, he mostly desires to have his own way. The best way to manage him was to ensure that he was supported to channel his energy positively e.g., get him to participate in engaging activities such as arranging puzzles. Joshua was a warm child and liked cuddles. He was indeed very fussy with his food in the sense that he mostly preferred junk food. Tola gave birth to him in London, United Kingdom. She gave birth to him five months after their arrival in the country.

When Joshua was about thirteen months old, Tola was able to do a short course in administration as a result of the encouragement and counselling she received from friends. Afterwards, she got an administrative job at the post office as a temporary staff. By this time Fred had secured a permanent job in the council. Two years later, Justin was given birth to. Justin was the fourth son of the family. He was very calm, and well developed for his age especially as he has a good understanding of many things. Tola gave birth to him in London, United Kingdom as well. Tola was able to work throughout his pregnancy, and his birthing process was relatively easy.

Tola's mum travelled to the UK to be with her and stayed with the family for about three months before she travelled back to Ibadan, Nigeria.

In the fourth year of residing in the UK, the Thomas' family applied for their 'Indefinite Leave to remain' and they were granted. As soon as the family got their 'Indefinite Leave to remain', Tola registered with Thames Mountain University to obtain her postgraduate studies in Finance and Risk management, so as to broaden her chance and scope for better job opportunities.

However, a few months into the course, the ugly incident of her children being placed in care started, and she had to drop out unfortunately. The stress of the family's ongoing challenges with the Social Services and the court proceedings is not describable.

During this period, Fred and Tola had confided in their church Pastor, who rallied round them with prayers and counselling. There was also Nkechi, their long-term friend, when they were working at the Tropical Chartered bank in Nigeria, who resides outside London, but works in London. She decided to spend two nights a week with them in order to keep them company. Sometimes Nkechi will bring 'take away' meals when she closes from work, so that Tola would not have to cook. Furthermore, intimate family members, both home, and abroad were informed of the development alongside Tola's mum, whom the children called Grandma.

She immediately began the arrangement to travel from Nigeria to the United Kingdom so as to support her daughter, and son in-law. It was indeed not her first time visiting the family since they relocated to the United Kingdom, as mentioned earlier, she was around for the birth of Justin.

To everything there is a season, A time for every purpose under heaven: **Ecclesiastes 3:1**

CHAPTER FIVE

It was December, a month after the children had been taken away from the only place they had known as home; the Social Services got in touch with Tola, and Fred through a Social Worker who introduced herself as Ruby. She told them she had been appointed as the children's social worker. She was from one of the African countries, but not a Nigerian. Even though the Social Services always prefer to pair people of the same ethnic origin together, it does not change anything for the people involved because the majority of the workers were just there to tick the boxes, and honestly, they cannot be blamed. Actually, they see work as just a means to an end, something that pays the bills and a way of keeping themselves occupied, and so they just roll along with it.

However, there are still some remnants that really want to make a difference. These sets of people recognise that they are dealing with real human beings, with real feelings, irrespective of their mistakes, or unfounded allegations. It should be emphasised here that the staff are dealing with people who have their whole future ahead of them, and whether or not they believe it, their input by way of write-ups, judgements, wrong conclusions, and negative attitude can have a longer lasting impact on their lives, destinies, and of course, the path they would eventually take in the future. The major gripe this particular Social Worker had with Tola and Fred was that they refused to acquiesce to what they had not done. Her own opinion was, "accept you are guilty, face the consequences" thereby wrapping up the whole process; job well done! Move on to the next victim. But how right was it to coerce someone into admitting to what he or she did not do, just for the sake of making a process go faster?

Remember that mindsets cannot be changed through force and coercion. No idea can be forcibly thrust upon any one.
Pervez Muharraf

Apparently, one of their children, Joshua, who was in reception class, had told his teacher that his parents beat him. What happened was that while he was changing for P.E in school, the teacher noticed some marks on his back, and the teacher, Miss Katie Young called him apart and asked him what had happened to his back. Joshua didn't respond and the teacher now went further by saying, "what does mummy do to you when you are naughty". She had already wrongly concluded that it was his parent that put the marks on his upper back. And the child answered that his parents beat him whenever he was being naughty. When they called his other siblings (Jameson and Jadon) in the same school for questioning, they also shared the same story that their parents beat them whenever they were naughty. Although no marks were found on their own bodies. Actually, the marks on Joshua's upper back were as a result of skin problems which the family GP was aware of, and made available to him an ongoing prescription cream for bathing, and moisturizing his skin.

Joshua was always scratching his back with his nails, because his skin was usually itchy. The Social Services further sent him to another specialist Doctor for more investigation about the mark. The Doctor reported that the type of marks was not consistent with beating, but agreed that it could be a skin problem, so the result was termed as inconclusive. Nevertheless, the fire had started already, and someone must pay for it! Neither the Social Services, nor the Police was going to get burned here, but someone else must take the blame, and in this case, it had to be the vulnerable parents, as it had been in many other cases.

All they wanted was for Fred, and Tola to agree that they had put the mark on their child, even though they had done nothing of such. Something that should have been resolved immediately was now dragged into over one year of going in and out of court! As Fred and Tola were dealing with the Social Services on one hand, they were also answering the Police officers on the other hand, resulting in months of attending Family and Criminal courts.

It is not as if both Tola and Fred don't discipline their children by correcting them with minimal smacking, but not with excessive force to the point of putting marks on their bodies. Their attitudes and beliefs about discipline stemmed from their own experiences of physical chastisement in early childhood, and adolescence. These experiences formed the basis of their approach to implementing guidance, boundaries, and discipline for their children. Fred is the fun dad who indulges, and spoils the children rotten. It's not even clear why his name was mentioned. While Tola on the other hand is only guilty of using the word 'beat' loosely around the children.

Any little thing she would say 'I will beat you', without really carrying out the real physical activity of beating, or smacking. It was like a threat to serve as a deterrent to stop the child from being naughty. But children soaked all these things up in their heads. And they started to use the same terminology too. Even Jameson uses the word 'beat' to discourage his younger ones from carrying out certain activities. Parents need to redefine their language around their children. Words spoken to children must be intentional, and purposeful. This will inevitably shape their characters.

Knife killing is a well-known phenomenon among the black children and youths in the city of London, having recently migrated to the country four years earlier, Fred and Tola started educating their children, at the early stage of their development, about the differences between wrong and right. It's unfortunate that some parents have caused harm to their own children to the point of killing them, but that was never Fred and Tola's intention.

These loving parents were only correcting their children in love, so that they can turn out well for themselves, family, community, and the nation at large. They wanted their children to turn out to be good people who are God-fearing, who do not follow the path of self-destruction, trouble and mischief, which sadly, many young children follow nowadays.

*Your greatest accomplishment may not be something you do but someone you raise. - **Andy Stanley***

.

CHAPTER SIX

Family is the building block of any great society. The way a family is built is very important, because the end result will reflect on the larger society. It is a known fact that there exists a brutal punishment which the western countries' criminal justice system metes out to offenders of African descent. Once the invisible line is crossed, the trouble starts, and you have no idea of when you are going to get out of this emotionally damaging trap. It hurts beyond words when you are wrongly accused, and you are not given any chance to explain yourself!

Contradictorily, parents are not allowed to discipline their children the way they believe could work for their family, but the society then disciplines the same children in a severe way when they grow up and become unruly. Is it not better to inculcate the fear of God, the norms, and acceptable societal behaviour in them when they are still young, and can still be moulded? It's a question that remains unanswered!

During this period, the maternal grandmother, Mrs Olushola, arrived from Nigeria to offer Fred and her daughter, Tola some of her love, and support. Her presence actually gave them some sort of hope, and stability. Initially it was as if the whole world was against them, even though they had each other to rely on, mountains are very lonely places.

Therefore, it was such a huge relief when Grandma arrived. Her arrival reminded them, and assured them of the strong support from their family members. Grandma continuously comforted them about the care, and concern from their family members who were rooting for them.

Prior to this moment, it was such a lonely place to be. Tola thought it was funny how quickly people could change towards you, when you find yourself in a difficult place. You'll think you know someone long enough. You'll think you can predict how they will come to your rescue in times of need, but the reality is, everyone portrays who they want to be, who they think others want them to be, especially if they stand to gain from you and while they are still gaining from you. Some even think you are getting what you so deserve, that your sin might just be catching up with you. Some think you'll probably never get out of your dilemma; they have forgotten that the only constant thing is change, nothing remains forever except the mercy of

God, that is indisputable. Things change, circumstances change, people change. However, there were also some wonderful Christian friends who made themselves available by praying, and constantly sending words of encouragement to assure, and reassure Fred and Tola that all would be well. Some of them even offered to accommodate the children, but the Local Authority turned them down.

Subsequently, a new Social Worker named, Lola Jacobs, was appointed for the children, after about three months of the children remaining in care. The four children had been settled with a culturally compatible woman, known as Aunt Bridget. Lola Jacobs was a Black British, from Nigeria. She went to visit the couple, and informed them that an upcoming supervised visit had been arranged for them with their children, and that it would be ongoing until the whole case was resolved. Lola was also not comfortable with the couple's 'not guilty' plea. She cited different episodes of children that have been taken into care and was of the opinion that the State, and the Local Authority are always on the side of the children.

Each time she came on a visit, she would always chant "you cannot win the Local Authority." She would chant it four to five times before she leaves. Tola was like oh yea, here we go again, "you can never win the Local Authority." She felt she needed to come up with her own chant too, "I will win the Local Authority." Tola decided to remain positive in spite of everything.

Not long after her visit, the supervised visitation began. Tola and Fred were scheduled to visit the children three times a week while they were being assessed by different contact supervisors throughout the entire period. Different places were used for the contact visits. Examples of which were the offices of the Local Authority, children's centre within the borough etc.

Some of the contact supervisors judged them and made their own conclusions just within the span of two hours, or thereabout of observing them with their children. Others were more amenable, and actually saw a father and a mother fighting for the wellbeing of their children, fighting for the future of their children, fighting for their family, and fighting for the institution called Marriage. The children were still very young (all four children were above fourteen months, and under ten years old), they didn't know or understand the consequences of what they had said about their parents. In fact, Jadon said it was like being on holiday. Although the mark was noticed on Joshua, the two older ones, Jameson and Jadon took full advantage of the situation; they were being chauffeur driven to and from school, they didn't need to do any little household chores etc.

However, they were still children. When one gives children an inch, they will take a mile. During the period of the children staying under the care of the state, they didn't have to go and stay with a childminder after school while they waited for their parents to pick them up. As mentioned earlier, the family had recently migrated to the UK not long before the episode took place. They were still struggling to find their bearing financially. The couple were working to support the family, and they had to employ the services of a childminder. Tola and Fred have always been a peace-loving couple who absolutely love and adore their children. This was invariably so as devout Christians, who gave birth to four children as a young couple.

The efforts and sacrifices that go into bringing up children in a foreign country, where helping hands were not commonly offered should be commended, unlike their own country where help was readily available from family and friends. For many years, they were not entitled to any child benefits; yet that did not stop their desire, and love to have four children. They always took their children to the church with other children where they were taught the ways of God, how to grow up to be responsible children of God, and to become responsible members of the society.

Tola worked as a locum staff with one of the Postal Services in the United Kingdom. She opted for a temporary job so as to have a bit of flexibility, while Fred's work was permanent. As a result of Fred's job commitment, he always arrived towards the end of the contact visit sessions and the children were always happy to see him. However, Tola and her mum (the children's grandma) were more than able to make up for any lapses in visitations. They took along with them well-prepared home meals for the children which Grandma made specially, including bean cakes. The children loved, and always enjoyed it.

To all of the grandmothers who make the world more gentle, more tolerant and safer for our children. Never doubt your importance. **Mary-Lou Rosengren**

CHAPTER SEVEN

It should be stated here that during this period many parents were victims of the Police and the Social Services' harassment. In fact, within the children's school alone, two other families of African descent also suffered this misfortune, and their children were taken into the care of Local Authorities. Broadyard Primary School in particular was allegedly being funded to do this, though it could not be substantiated.

Apparently, a major incident had occurred before that period, where a couple killed their own child. Thus, the school felt they were doing their due diligence to safeguard the children, because of the children's disclosure. In as much as it is good to know that the school, and the State are looking out for the plight of the vulnerable, especially children, this particular case was totally different considering the fact that the teachers knew the parents well, and that they never missed any of their children's parent's evenings. Tola attended reading classes with the children, and also attended the school's Christmas concerts. Fred and Tola were clearly involved in all the children's school activities. All their children started from the Nursery of that same school, apart from the eldest, Jameson, who started from the Reception year.

The same Teacher, Miss Katie Young, who taught their eldest son, Jameson in Reception year was also the Teacher that was teaching Joshua in his Reception year. She was the one that noticed the mark on his back. Miss Katie Young was the first Teacher Tola met on her arrival to Broadyard school, which incidentally was the first school they attempted in the United Kingdom to register their children.

Tola could recollect very well when she went to register Jameson in the school, he was put in the reception year, due to his age, and Miss Young welcomed Jameson and Tola very warmly. Tola told her husband later that day that Miss Katie Young must be a Christian because she had said to her, "God bless you", as she was leaving her class. Their kids were well known in the school, and they were brilliant pupils. Unfortunately, during this difficult period, the school, including the teachers, treated them like strangers and criminals. The kids had hundred percent attendance, and all their medical records about immunization were up to date. All four of their children were always well presented, and articulate. This ought to be seen as a credit based on the quality of parenting they had received in the hands of both Fred and Tola.

Tola had always taken the children to the doctors whenever required, and had ensured that the children went to school every weekday. Consequently, their academic performances were usually above average. This cannot be said to be the typical behaviour of parents who neglect their children or beat them up. If Tola was beating up her children as alleged, she would not allow them out in public, or allow them to engage with professionals such as teachers and doctors. However, neither the Police, nor the Social Services took these into consideration when dealing with them. All they saw was a black family trying to make ends meet. They refused to acknowledge that they were just a regular and caring family trying to love, provide for, and set good examples for their children.

Guess what? Your position in society, the colour of your skin, and the job you do could be grounds for people to judge you. That was exactly what happened in the case of Fred and Tola. After this discovery, Tola and Fred decided to seek legal counsel, and applied for legal aid, which was granted to them fortunately. Each of them had two Lawyers representing them in both criminal, and family proceedings. The Local Authority brought charges of neglect, which were being handled at the Family Court, while the Police brought charges of assault of minors, which were being handled at the Crown Court. Both charges however ran concurrently. Consequently, as they were attending the Family court, they were also attending the Crown Court, although on different dates.

They also had to visit the children at the contact centres. At the beginning of the criminal case proceedings, they appeared at the Magistrate Court, where Fred and Tola pleaded, "not guilty." And the case was referred to the Crown court. When Tola initially met with the Lawyer representing her for the criminal proceedings, who happened to come from one of the African countries-Ghana to be precise, he gave her lots of hope, saying he had experienced a similar situation with his own children.

According to him, one of his children had allegedly reported him to one of his teachers in the school about being physically abused, but the case was quickly nipped in the bud before it got out of hand most especially when the school realised that they were dealing with a Lawyer. He was so confident that there would be no need to go to trial, and they would sue the Police and the Local authority for all the trouble they made them go through.

The Lawyer's story gave them hope, and lightened their burdens. Hope is a seed that could bloom all too quickly when its host is so eager to feed it. Little did they know that their brouhaha was just starting. The Police were relentless, and brutal in their pursuit of the case. It was like giving a bone to a dog, and it refuses to let it go. That was exactly the way the Police behaved. They knew it would not augur well for them if they lost, because of the way they had handled the whole case.

They were not ready to be victims, but were ready to make Fred and Tola victims by destroying their family, and sending them to prison. It was when the second criminal Lawyer representing Fred, who happened to be from Nigeria, (though Black British), was brought in, that they (Fred and Tola) began to realise the kind of problem they were in. Apparently, the Police had interviewed the two eldest children, Jameson and Jadon on tape, where they asked the children the mode of discipline their parents employed whenever they were naughty, and the Police were going to use all these against the parents during trial. Even though their criminal Lawyers made the tape available to them, Fred and Tola refused to watch it.

In spite of their refusal, their Lawyers briefed them about what was inside the tape; which included asking children to kneel down in a corner, smacking them on their bum, threatening to beat them, without actually going through with it most of the time etc. All of these were prevalent within the black community anyway. Those were the methods of discipline Fred and Tola's parents used on them which they also adopted. They never intended to cause harm to any of their children, but the way the Police went about it was like they were criminals who had brought hardship upon their own children. This narrative was not true at all. Actually, where Fred and Tola came from, children are the joy and the pride of their parents. Most parents invest heavily in their children. This viewpoint influenced the desire of Fred and Tola to relocate to the United Kingdom; an advanced country, to give their children something better towards the future.

If a wise man contends with a foolish man, Whether the fool rages or laughs, there is no peace. **Proverbs 29:9**

CHAPTER EIGHT

The Foster Carer, Aunt Bridget had confirmed that the marks on Joshua were due to medical condition as she herself noticed fresh marks on his body while in her care. She decided to take him to the hospital for a blood test, and the doctor that examined him said the marks were as a result of his dry skin condition. Therefore, the Police could no longer use the excuse of marks on Joshua's back, but then, they focused mainly on what Jameson and Jaden had said about smacking them.

By this time, most friends and family members, from far and near had gotten to know what was happening. Some even felt offended that they were not informed earlier. One of Tola's Aunties, whose son was a family Lawyer also rallied round them; he was even willing to put himself forward to accommodate the children, so that the children could be with family members.

Tola's brother, Tunji, and his wife also supported them. Tola's younger sister Tolu that lived in Nigeria was so concerned and bothered by the whole situation. Fred's younger brother, Steve tried to take his annual leave earlier to travel to the United Kingdom in order to support his brother, and wife, but his place of work did not grant him early leave.

Various people were coming up with different ideas, and advice, just to assist the family. Negative situations in life can erode confidence, it will chip away one's self-worth. Such a person will look like a fool, who does not know anything. Even people who ought not to know your business will begin to offer you advice, but it is not everyone that should know about your pain and not everyone is really interested in your pain anyway. Notwithstanding, it is still reasonable to be vulnerable with the right people. A dear friend of Tola, who attended another Pentecostal denomination from her own church advised her that the problem with the local authority could not be handled in her (Tola's) church and she invited Tola to her own church but Tola refused because she knew whom she had believed.

A believer does not have to run from pillar to post when challenges of life arise. God has the backs of all His children; A child of God is a carrier of God's presence by the power of the Holy Spirit. There is no need to start running from one church to another seeking what is not lost. That is the reason the word of God encourages people to pray without ceasing. And when challenges of life come, a believer will still be able to radiate the peace of God because he or she has always been in communion with the heavenly Father. There was an incident that happened during one of the contact visits. While Tola was waiting for the children to arrive, a strange woman engaged her in conversation, this woman told her that she also had a similar problem in the past. According to her, although it was her niece, not her child, who reported her to the Police and Social Services, and therefore had to engage the service of a woman who prayed for her during her travail. There and then, she called the woman for Tola to speak with her. However, Tola's spirit did not agree with that of the woman. That notwithstanding, Tola was respectful, and she thanked the woman, but did not follow up with any of them.

Fred and Tola did not relent in their services to God and to their local Church assembly. Fred, a leader in the church, continued to carry out his assignment to God through the church. Tola recalled the Pastor's wife commending her that she was really doing well despite what was happening. A specific incident that stayed with Tola during the whole challenging period was an occasion during Fred's birthday celebration, when the pastor's wife surprised them by bringing a cake to the church for Fred to cut on his birthday. This act of kindness brought them some happiness. Fred and Tola went out to a restaurant later by themselves to celebrate, and also to reflect on the happenings around them. At some point in life, a person grows into himself. It's like discovering oneself afresh and thereafter, one determines or proposes how to move forward henceforth. The decision is not static though, it will keep on evolving with new experiences of life especially as God has given everyone the freedom of choice.

Tola and her husband decided to trust their heavenly Father, God, to see them through. She had given her life to Jesus Christ at an early age, secondary school precisely, and she had always recognised God as her Father, while Fred committed his life to Christ after his university degree. Thus, they knew whom they had placed their faith upon, the only living God who does all things well, and always on time. They knew fully well that only God could help them, so they trusted Him, and prayed to Him alone. The church leadership they belonged to at the time also lifted them up in prayers, and with encouraging words. Although there were lots of whisperings behind their backs, they remained firm in their faith. Both of them were very private, and conservative personalities, so they disclosed as little as possible, but people just made up their own stories along the way as usual.

Do not hide Your face from me in the day of my trouble; Incline Your ear to me; In the day that I call, answer me speedily. **Psalm 102:2**

CHAPTER NINE

As the children were under the care of the State, they bought them a lot of clothes, toys, shoes etc. and further promised them lots of Christmas gifts. Consequently, when the children were asked if they wanted to return home, they said yes but not until after Christmas. They were indeed being pampered, and since they knew that they were under the protection of the State, they thought they could do whatever they liked. Furthermore, the children were aware of the fact that each contact was being observed, and the supervisors were taking notes, they sometimes got carried away and played up, by not wanting to adhere to set boundaries from their parents.

They got carried away by all the attention they were receiving from different agencies. There was this blatant disregard for authority to the point of rudeness, and when Tola called them out on it during one of the contact visits, they also used that as ammunition against her. If parents fail to properly set boundaries for their children, the negative consequences will eventually come to them in the future, especially in the light of the recent knife killing among the youth in the United Kingdom.

Parents should be parents, and they should be allowed to live up to their responsibilities of providing a conducive environment for their children to thrive in, love them and still not be afraid to correct them when they do something wrong. It is because they have their best interest at heart that they took out time to instil discipline in them so that the system will not eventually have to punish them (the children) in the future. It is true that parents might not always be right, but the constant sure thing is that every rational parent wants the best for their children.

Most parents learn on the job, one cannot apply the same rule for every child because of their differences/ uniqueness in makeup. That makes parenthood to be a work in progress.

Their foster carer, Aunt Bridget even assented to the fact that, of all the children she had looked after, they were the most well-behaved children. It was a credence to part of the parents' nurturing capability. Children are wiser and better off obeying their parents, through the precepts and counsel of the word of God. Contrary to the Police officer's statement earlier in the book, that she was aware that parents from Nigeria maltreat their children, they actually take delight in sharing their children's achievements, they are always proud of them. There were several pictures that were taken that bore credence to this; different pictures showing the children's celebrations both in Nigeria, and the United Kingdom; family holidays in Nigeria, birthday party celebrations, sports days, happy times at home, family getting ready to go to church, family outings, and lunch, graduation from nursery and reception, children in their school wear ready to go to School etc.

Fred and Tola marked their birthdays by throwing parties for them, bought them gifts, and took them out to enjoy themselves. Tola's brother, Tunji with his wife Linda, and their children always showered them with love each time they visited them during the holidays. Tolu, Tola's younger sister who resided in Nigeria paid a designer to make beautiful African native attires for the children which she thereafter dispatched to them via courier so as to make them happy. The children's friends were allowed to come over to the house. As a matter of fact, one of the children loved to host and entertain his friends in the house.

Fred and Tola really value the education of their children so much that they invested a lot of money on an after-school program which was called: The Student Support Centre Programme, and it involved different

Teachers teaching the children on different topics in Maths and English via DVD. It also came along with textbooks. The parents were being debited directly every month for the lessons despite the fact that money was tight, but that was the level of sacrifice they made for their children.

Tola derives so much pleasure and happiness in sacrificing her own comfort and happiness for the children, which by the way she will repeat again, if it comes down to it. She loves her children very much. Four months after the children were put into care, a referral was received from the children's school, stating that Joshua had disclosed that he was scared of his foster carer. Joshua was reported to have alleged that the foster carer, Aunt Bridget, held his cheeks, threw him down, asked him to sit on the stairs and also sent him to his room. It was later agreed that the matter would be dealt with by the Care Standards. By this time all the four children had become restless, and wanted to return back home.

Moreover, they had realised the consequences of their misleading disclosure. At the end of every contact session, Joshua will hold on tight to his father's leg, crying and saying he wants to go home. It was always a heart-breaking moment. He didn't fully understand why his grandmother, father and mother would visit him and his siblings at the contact centre, and only for them to leave him there without taking him home with them. Exactly a month after Joshua's disclosure about the foster carer, a phone call was received from Broadyard primary school where Joshua made further disclosure that the foster carer beat him, and asked him to kneel on the floor. Joshua also disclosed that she (the foster carer) asked him to say strange words. The Headteacher, Mr Alexandra stated, Joshua had said in the school that he was not happy, and does not want to be in his current placement, but rather wishes to return home.

It was the same Headteacher who called the Social Services, and the Police on the parents instead of speaking with them first. As a result of Joshua's disclosure, the Local Authority made a decision to move the children to another home, but Fred and Tola vehemently refused the uprooting of the children again. They explained that Joshua usually plays up whenever he does not get his own way. Fortunately, the family liaison officer supported the parents' viewpoint that the children should not be moved from their current placement.

During this period, various assessments, reports from professionals like the Guardian, Social Services, and Foster Carer had highlighted that Jameson, Jadon and Joshua had repeatedly agitated that they would like to return to the care of their parents. Justin's wishes and feelings could not be ascertained due to his age, and level of understanding. However, his parents regularly assured him that everything would soon be over. Jameson in particular had consistently expressed bewilderment at the length of time he and his siblings have had to reside in care.

Correct your son, and he will give you rest; Yes, he will give delight to your soul. ***Proverbs 29:17***

CHAPTER TEN

By now the children had remained in care for seven months, and the local authority contemplated releasing them into the care of their grandmother. What that meant was that Tola and her husband would have to move out of the family home. The reason being that grandma will take care of the children in a familiar environment. Aside from this, the house was very close to the children's school, and their friend's home. There was a possibility that if this became a reality, it would gradually begin to help the children to return back to normality.

Therefore, a viability assessment of Tola's mum was carried out by an independent Social Worker, Mrs Ada Tonkeh, who was culturally appropriate, and had an insight to what transpired in the West African societies. There were no concerns about grandma's insight and understanding of the children's basic care needs. Her emotional warmth, and affection obviously reflected during observed contact visits with the children.

Furthermore, grandma's parenting skills/experiences were considered, as she had raised six children of her own through to adulthood. It is noteworthy to emphasise that all grandma's children were University graduates, and married with children of their own. She also had fifteen grandchildren as at then and had regular contacts with them all. Grandma happened to be a qualified Nurse, and Midwife with considerable experience, and seniority within the profession before she retired. However, her response to the specific and emotional needs of the children was considered to be a challenge as a result of the number of children involved, coupled with their different ages and stages of development. In view of this, she was turned down.

Thereafter, Grandma decided to go back home to Nigeria. However, before she eventually travelled back, Fred and Tola still ensured that she enjoyed her stay even though it was very challenging and difficult. She loved going out every Friday night to eat 'isi ewu' (a local Nigerian delicacy) which usually relaxes her, especially as she suffered from high blood pressure. The couple was always careful not to aggravate her health by occasionally taking her out to relax. She also loved watching documentaries about the Royal family, especially the Queen. Someone who does not know her would probably think that she went to the same school with the Queen mostly with regards to the way and manner whereby she talked about the Queen. She was so fascinated about the Royal family, particularly, the Queen. Granma advised Tola and Fred to continue to cooperate with all the professionals who were working with them. She further said, "there is nothing too much to give up for one's children, do not worry about the ridicule now, this is the time to endure and sacrifice."

They thereafter hugged, and drove her to the airport so as to catch her flight. As time went on, another Social Worker by the name Anton who hailed originally from the Caribbean was allocated to the children. He was a real professional, who seemed to know what he was doing, and the children also liked him. He was very surprised that they had dragged the matter for so long. He carried out his responsibility with a sense of urgency, but at the same time was quite sensitive to the parents' plight. He was such an easy-going person, and a delight to relate with.

The parents continued to visit their children under the supervision of the Local Authority, but they were not making a headway concerning resolving the problem at hand which related to the children returning back home. The reason being that they had simply refused to own up to the allegation of putting a mark on their boy. The police too refused to back down, and they decided to go to trial. The parents on their own part also felt that there was nothing they could do other than going to trial.

Consequently, the Criminal Lawyers started preparing their clients for trial. Friends and family members were asked to write statements of witness to support the couple. Many friends were happy to oblige but Fred and Tola were somehow surprised when one of their friends began to play pranks. However, in hindsight, they eventually understood why that particular friend was reluctant to write them a letter.

Apparently, she had an issue which was beyond her capacity to handle. She needed to protect herself, which was quite understandable. Nevertheless, friends and family members like Yvonne, their friend, and neighbour, Nkechi who had known the couple since their days in Tropical Chartered Bank in Nigeria, their local parish Pastor, Tola's sister in-law, Linda, friends from the church, to list just a few wrote excellent letters to testify to the integrity of Tola and Fred. Moreover, the God-fearing attributes of these young parents alongside their exemplary qualities as a couple, and as a close-knit family stood out prominently in their statement of witness.

During this period, Fred and Tola's relationship with their children had taken a good turn. The children were tired of remaining in the care system, and they wanted to return home. They even went to the extent of changing their stories with regards to what they had told the Police, but the whole issue was already out of their hands. It was time to prepare for the trial, and not fret about what the children had disclosed. One cannot afford to worry about a stable door when the horse had already bolted, neither was it time to give up. What story would be told in the future? An adage says "You don't have to climb a tree to see the future."

Africans value family relationships to the extent that they practice a system of communal living. A parent cannot take her children to court, neither can the children take their parents to court. Because if either lost, all lost. It's a family thing, it will change the dynamics of the whole relationship, thereby negatively impacting the family life. Family should be based on the principles of love, respect, forgiveness and tolerance. All these virtues will enable families to thrive and the society will be better for it as against one that is destroyed by the intrusion of external forces in the name of protecting vulnerable people. Whatever decision is being made now would have a longer lasting impact on the future of the whole family.

Mrs Anand, the Children's guardian introduced community activities to the contact visitations, and the contact visits were also increased from three times a week to four times a week, including weekends. As against restriction of the children within the confinement of the Social Services' office, or rooms in the community centres, various outing activities were incorporated by the children's guardian. The role of the guardian was to look out for the best interests of the children, and ensure that their needs were met. Furthermore, her role was like check and balance on the activities of the local authority. Her genuineness, and interest towards resolving the case and thereafter reuniting the family shone across. She actually lived up to her role, by facilitating the process. Rather than meeting at the contact centres, she would follow the parents, and the children to have meals at restaurants, while at the same time carrying out her job of assessing the parents alongside their children.

The community activities (swimming, going for picnics in the park, going to the leisure centre, going to restaurants for meals at the weekends etc.) actually gave the children and their parents the opportunity to spend quality time together, and they enjoyed the special time (although restricted, but was very meaningful, and well planned). It allowed the parents to enjoy child- focused activities with their children, and further fostered a healthier attachment between the children, and the parents.

On a particular occasion, the parents took the children for swimming at the sport centre during one of their supervised contact visits. Fred participated fully in the activity and swam with the children in the pool. Jameson was swimming in the bigger pool while Fred was swimming with Jadon and Joshua in the smaller pool. He taught them how to kick in the pool and also how to embark on floating and back strolling. They later moved to the bigger pool, where Fred played handball games with three of the children. It was really fun, and the children were very happy. They enjoyed their dad's company as well as the swimming activity. Tola sat in the spectator's gallery with Justin, watching them while she looked after Justin who refused to swim. The whole family later sat together for snacks (cakes, drinks, sweets, etc). On the whole, the children were happy, and everybody enjoyed the outing. At the end of that particular contact, Tola and Fred hugged the children affectionately while saying goodbye, and they asked them what they would like to be done for them during the next contact visit.

Something else was happening at the other side- the Criminal Court case was ongoing. During one of the pre-trial meetings at the Crown court, the judge threatened to send the couple to jail. He said, "you must be joking if you think you are going to avoid a custodial sentence". Both criminal Lawyers representing the parents were so infuriated by the threat of the judge, they were beside themselves with anger. Nonetheless, Fred and Tola remained calm throughout the proceedings, without betraying any emotion. All they wanted was for their children to be returned to their custody as they were not having any dispute with their children but rather, the system. The judge must have been carried away! Who does that? Was that even professional at all?

A popular adage says that "there is more hope for a fool than one who speaks in haste during a court proceeding, for he does not even know the outcome of the trial as it could go either way". The particular case had not gone to trial, and the judge was already threatening, even without the jury's input. Someone would have thought it's only in developing countries that the presiding judge sees himself as alpha and omega.

Apparently, it happens in developed nations too! More often than not, this probably had to do with the type and class of people such a judge was dealing with. In this case, the judge actually appointed himself as both the judge, and the jury. Fred and Tola's Lawyers were also of the opinion that the jury in that locality were likely to be biased, especially when one considers the colour of the couple's skin. There was a likelihood that most of the jury panel would come from the environment where the trial was taking place, which was predominantly a white dominated area, and they might not fully understand the culture of the couple. As a result, the criminal Lawyers proposed that the family settle out of court.

The judge at the family court was more amenable, he indeed presided over the case with kindness, and understanding. He would on several occasions make positive suggestions that will bring about an amicable resolution of the whole matter. He was probably a grandfather who genuinely knew that these parents truly love their children, even though the mode of disciplining their children was not acceptable in the United Kingdom, however such a mode of discipline will not raise an eyebrow in their own country of origin. The family Lawyer working with Fred was very positive, he was actually the first lawyer the family contacted at the beginning of the problem. According to him he couldn't have imagined that the whole case would escalate to the level it eventually reached.

However, he was always positive and supportive. He never believed that anything was impossible and "where there's a will there will always be a way". Tola and Fred came face to face with Miss Katie Young during one of the family court proceedings. She indeed looked undecided, but Tola said hello to her, and she replied back politely. Fred was even angry that Tola greeted her, but as children of God, one cannot afford to bear a grudge. Your heavenly Father would forgive you, when you forgive people who offend you.

As a matter of fact, Tola did wonder whether or not Miss Katie Young ever regretted reporting her to the Police and Local Authority. Obviously, she now understood the difference between when Joshua was living at home with his parents, and when he had been living in foster care. Joshua who used to be a young boisterous boy full of life had now suddenly turned to an attention-seeking, clinging boy who throws tantrums in class.

The incident, and the experience of being placed in the care of a Local Authority affected him the most.

Nonetheless, his parents endeavoured to show him love, understanding, and a reassurance that everything would be fine. Considering Justin's age, he did remarkably well. He was able to adapt well to all the professionals who were working with the family. Some of the Social Workers even commented that he could have been adopted because of his age, and the longevity of the care proceedings.

The probability that we may fail in the struggle ought not to deter us from the support of a cause we believe to be just.
- Abraham Lincoln

CHAPTER ELEVEN

Following the rejection of Mrs Olushola's assessment (the maternal grandmother) with regards to whether or not she was fit to take custody of the children, the same independent Social Worker, Mrs Ada Tonkeh was asked to carry out an assessment on Fred and Tola if they were suitable enough for the children to return to their care. She was professional, but at the same time showed some form of humanity. She had different sessions with them over a period of one month. Some sessions were with Tola alone, while some were with Fred. They also had some joint sessions with her. She even on some occasions visited the children, and talked with them. She also assessed the parents' interaction with the children at the contact centre.

According to the Independent social worker's report, she took into consideration the Right of Respect for

Family Life in accordance with the Human Rights Act 1998, and also explored whether the parents as a couple can make the necessary changes that would facilitate the children's return back to their care. When she had subsequently reviewed all the paperwork made available to her from the courts, and the professionals involved in the case, she came to a conclusion that the case was clearly family support oriented.

Meaning Fred and Tola should be supported, and educated to make the necessary changes that will facilitate their children's return back to their custody; and thereafter provide them with ongoing training that will enable them to parent their children safely, and appropriately without resorting to physical chastisement. She also observed that the four children had experienced unnecessarily prolonged separation from their parents as a result of the punitive stance of the Police, and the Local Authority. Furthermore, the independent Social Worker advised that the children were better off released to the custody of both Tola and Fred. She also suggested that the Local Authority should work with the parents on a gradual process of getting the children back home.

During the sessions, the independent Social Worker discussed with Tola about her feelings concerning the ongoing criminal, and child care proceedings. She explored her family background, and history, her relationship with her husband, her experiences when she was under the custody of her parents including the kind of discipline she received from her parents as well as her parents' relationship with one another. The independent social worker, Mrs Ada Tonkeh also looked into Tola's educational, and work experience background. She did the same with Fred as well.

Tola learned a lot and the experience was not palatable at all. She was raised in an environment where smacking a child was acceptable, and not classified as cruelty. Her parents were loving parents who always had her best interest at heart, but their own method of setting boundaries included smacking, though not excessive, and there was no history of domestic abuse between her parents. Tola loves her children very much, and as far as she is concerned, they are her world. She wants the best for them, she misses them very much, and worries about them all the time, especially as she felt that she was missing out on their development during their formative years. She gave up a lot to relocate to the United Kingdom.

The main reason for her relocation was because of her children, so that they could have the best opportunities in life. Since this incident, she had learnt a number of parenting techniques (via watching supernanny on TV, carrying out research activities on parenting, and during sessions with Independent Social Worker) to set appropriate boundaries for her children. She has also realised that it is important to learn the Laws of the country of your residence, so that you don't fall foul of them as an immigrant but strictly abide by them. It should be emphasized that "ignorance is not an excuse in Law". For instance, insinuations such as "this is the way my parents trained me, it's the way of our culture" etc will not hold water when the arm of the law of the land catches up with you"

Fred also found the whole experience very challenging, and extremely difficult. He did learn a lot, and acquired the kind of knowledge he could not have bought with money, or read in a book. More importantly, this knowledge had further enriched him as a father; he now seems to see things from other people's perspective, and has a deeper understanding of the system in the United Kingdom. Fred's intentions are good, and his motives are right toward his children, which was the major reason why he corrected them. Moreover, he usually endeavoured to teach them the difference between right and wrong. He loves his children with passion. He is aware now that there are other ways to put boundaries in place for children, and offer guidance to them. In addition to this current knowledge, he keeps learning and developing every day.

Even though this current learning had been tough, "learning is learning" and Fred will be a better parent for it. He now knows about various parenting strategies, and how to set, and enforce boundaries. Despite the fact that the entire care proceedings have been hard on the family, it indeed brought Fred and Tola closer together. They have been able to appreciate themselves better and they refused to cast blame on each other. Their romantic life was also better for it. When the Independent Social Worker finished her work, and subsequently submitted her findings, and recommendations in favour of the children being returned back to the custody of their parents, the Local Authority still refused to release the children; they thought the parents were going to blame their children for the disclosure.

However, there was never a situation where the parents blamed their children for the disclosure, but rather they blamed the system. The children were young and they had behaved as children, but the authorities should not have dragged the matter to the extreme, which unfortunately, they did. The Local Authority then brought in another Independent Social Worker, who also arrived at the same findings, conclusion, and recommendation like the first independent social worker. Actually, the second independent social worker further emphasised that the way and manner whereby the parents disciplined their children was not unusual among the black community.

It should however be said that even though both independent social workers hailed from Nigeria, and they both understood Nigerian culture very well, under no circumstances did they support the parents' mode of disciplining their children. Notwithstanding anyway, they maintained a stand that the children are safe with their parents.

Despite the various and different sessions, the second independent social worker had with the parents, it did not seem as if a solution to the problem was in sight, especially as the children continued to stay longer in care than the parents envisaged. They missed many family celebrations like birthdays, Christmas celebrations, and Easter celebrations. At this point in time, the children had started missing home, and they then realised the enormity of their disclosure but unfortunately, it was out of their hands as the ball was now in the court of the Police and the Local Authority.

When obstacles arise, you change your direction to reach your goal, you do not change your decision to get there.
- Zig Ziglar

CHAPTER TWELVE

Whenever the parents went for contact visits, the two youngest children- Joshua and Justin would cry and hold on to their parents. On several occasions, they even completely refused to go back to their foster carer. Jameson and Jadon were better able to control their emotions but they were equally distraught with how the whole matter lingered. It was always an emotional period for the family to the extent that one of the contact supervisors burst into tears when she saw how the entire family was being frustrated.

Specifically, one could remember a particular episode when Joshua said to his parents; "I will behave well and not cry, perhaps they would allow me to go home, mummy?" With all these incidents, the parents would never understand how the Local Authority could ever believe they were helping such a child by removing him from the care of his biological parents who love him dearly. Simultaneously, the criminal Lawyers were in serious deliberation with the Prosecuting Counsel, and both sides eventually agreed to settle out of court, based on agreement concerning certain terms and conditions. At this juncture, both Fred and Tola were compelled to agree with the Authority's accusation of smacking their two oldest children, Jameson and Jadon with flip flop slippers occasionally, as an offence.

The prosecutor then decided not to proceed with the case against the parents with regards to putting marks on Joshua's back, some compromise on both sides were consequently reached.

Furthermore, both the Police and the Local Authority agreed that the family (children and parents) should be reunited together, but that it should follow a gradual process. When Fred and Tola learnt that the children would be coming home, it was music to their ears, and they were both thrilled to bits. Consequently, a timetable was drawn up by Anton i.e., the children's Social Worker concerning how the children would return home over a period of three weeks which would be in batches, beginning with the youngest children, Joshua and Justin, and to be followed a day later by the two oldest children, Jameson and Jadon.

For I have placed the sand as a boundary for the sea, an eternal decree and a perpetual barrier beyond which it cannot pass. Though the waves [of the sea] toss and break, yet they cannot prevail [against the sand ordained to hold them back]; Though the waves and the billows roar, yet they cannot cross over [the barrier]. [Is not such a God to be feared?] **Jeremiah 5:22**

It is a known truth that every problem has its expiration date. God has ordained life in such a way that challenges will not go beyond the time, and season He has allowed or permitted. If people know this, they will fret less, and trust God more for He is the one who knows the end from the beginning. When the appointed time of favour dawned, every hand was on deck to facilitate the return of the children back home. The Police decided not to go further with the case. The Local Authority, and all the professionals agreed that the children had stayed out of their home for too long. This happened because it was time for strength to be released from captivity.

When strength is about to be released from captivity, negative reports will no longer matter, following up on parenting classes will not be remembered, the Police will have clarity of mind that they were just punishing the family unjustly, and it will suddenly dawn on the Local Authority: "this ought to have been resolved long time, it shouldn't have been dragged this long." Starting from the beginning of the subsequent week, Tola was permitted to be involved in the children's school run, she picked them from school and accompanied them to the foster carer's home throughout the week.

She then collected them from the foster carer's home in order for them to spend a whole Saturday with her and Fred. Thereafter, she would return them back in the evening. During this period, Fred's younger brother, Steve had also arrived from Nigeria with his family to spend his annual leave with the couple. Everybody was excited to see one another. The atmosphere was filled with excitement, and expectations.

The following week, the children spent the whole weekend with their parents, and afterwards Tola took them back to the foster carer on Sunday evening. With regards to the last week, and on the last day, both Tola and Fred brought the two youngest children Joshua and Justin home, a day earlier before the two eldest children Jameson and Jadon were brought home. The children were raring to go home, they simply couldn't wait. All the children were so excited to be back home. While on their way home on the day they were finally released, Tola could remember Justin saying, "Joshua is my best friend forever."

The four children returned back home on the 21st of November 2012, exactly thirteen months after they left for school on a bright sunny, though chilly morning. The kind of wisdom the children have learned during their care experience, the parents couldn't have taught them by themselves.

Before that experience, the children were gullible, and

naive. However, they had now realised that there was no one more in their corner than their parents, and they are now aware of how valuable and precious they are as children to their parents.

They returned home safely and sound. The whole family continued to flourish. All the glory be to God.

He also brought them out with silver and gold, and there was none feeble among His tribes. **Psalm 105:37**

EPILOGUE

Inasmuch as it is good to know that there are institutions like the State, the Police, and the Local Authority that are looking out for children, and other vulnerable people, these institutions took this unique case to the extreme. In fact, one of the Lawyers told the parents that the case was diabolical, that it should not have reached the stage the Police escalated it to. Grandma travelled back to the United Kingdom from Nigeria to visit the children after they had returned home.

She also later visited the whole family on two different occasions before she went on to be with the Lord. The children always remember the important roles she played in their lives. The whole family applied for their British citizenship, and they were all granted. Tola also went back to school to complete her Master's Degree. The children don't really like their parents referring to their time in the care system, but it was part of their journey in life, and there should be no shame about it. Actually, they should see themselves as victors, and not victims. Indeed, God sees everyone in the light of the revelation of His words; therefore, other people's judgements, and opinions should not define one.

Thank God for the existence of the Care System, where hundreds of children have found refuge, but it is not every family that needs the Institution as some families need to be helped, and restored back together quickly. This particular family being spoken about surely did not need the care system. It is a known fact that the family still has good days and bad days occasionally where they shout at one another, slam the door, and speak in anger. Yet, is that enough to break up the family? Capital No. Nobody chose the family they were born into, God did.

The children are allowed to express their opinions when it comes to decision making, however it is still the parents that make the eventual final decision.

It should be further emphasised that as long as one lives in a depraved world, there will always be offence, friction, and misunderstanding as a result of people's uniqueness, and individuality. Words spoken in anger cannot be retracted, yet it must still be forgiven. And it is not a one-off thing but rather, it is as long as one lives. "Against You, You alone have I sinned" Psalm 51:4. Regardless of how often, and how deeply you have fallen, or how badly you have failed, God extends to you today, His grace, and a chance to begin again, if you are willing to accept it.

If God could bestow His grace upon humanity, then His children must extend the same grace to whoever offends them. God keeps showering His love on His creatures every day. Consequently, children of God must not only shower this type of love on their children, but also everyone they have contact with, or else love will not thrive, and it will eventually die.

Finally, even though it cannot be overemphasized that the United Kingdom is a great nation which looks after its vulnerable citizens and provides them with a fantastic care system, notwithstanding, any intervention of the State between parents and children should be proportionate to the legitimate aim of protecting family life, and not be a punitive measure or action.

And the ransomed of the LORD shall return, And come to Zion with singing, With everlasting joy on their heads. They shall obtain joy and gladness, And sorrow and sighing shall flee away. **Isaiah 35:10**